Written by
Hiroshi Osada

Illustrated by
Ryōji Arai

Translated from the Japanese by
David Boyd

Look, it's raining.

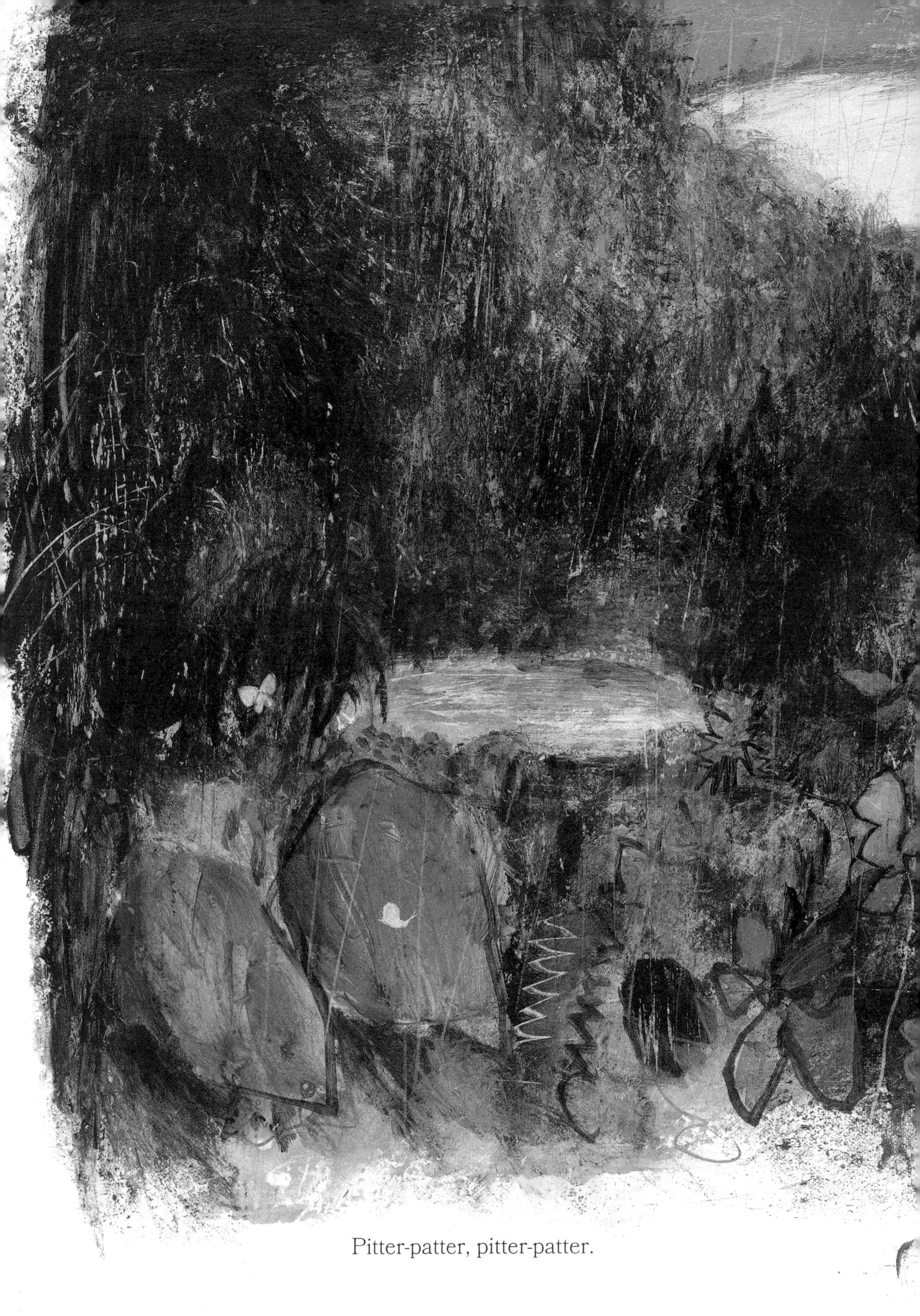

Pitter-patter, pitter-patter.

The rain gets louder.

Wetter and wetter, the blues darken.

So do the greens.

The wind whips, the rain slants.

Heavier and heavier, the rain gets louder now.

Cracking and crashing, the thunder roars.

Boom, bah-bah-BOOM!

Inevitably, lightning strikes.

Colors run across the leaves and swirl in the wind.

Whoosh, swish, sssh.

Just as quickly, it's over.
Look, no more rain.

Shimmering, light fills the sky.

The blues are blue again, and the greens are green.

Slowly, the air clears.

Slowly, all becomes bright.

Raindrops drip from the leaves.

Sparkling like crystals, they fall to the ground.

Setting, the light turns everything golden.

Stilling, the water shines silver.

A beautiful evening spreads across the sky.

It settles over the mountaintops.

There you are, white moon! And you, first star I see tonight.

The birds return home as shadows darken beneath the trees.

Falling, night fills the sky.

Flickering, the stars begin to sparkle.

After the rain, the sky is full of stars.

Shining, they share their stories.

Goodnight, Spirit of Rain, glowing in the sky.

The bunnies hop into the bright white moon.

We're all
falling
falling
soundly
soundly
asleep
asleep...

Hiroshi Osada was born in Fukushima City in 1939. He graduated from Waseda University in 1963. Two years later, he debuted as a poet with *This Journey*. In 1982, he received the Mainichi Publishing Culture Award for *The Bookstore of the Century*. In 1991, he won the Robō-no-ishi Literary Prize. In 1998, Osada was awarded the first Kuwabata Takeo Prize for *The Making of Memories*. In 2000, his collaboration with Ryōji Arai, *A Forest Picture Book*, earned the Kōdansha Publishing Culture Award for Children's Literature. His second collaboration with Ryōji Arai, *Every Color of Light*, followed. He died in 2015.

Ryōji Arai was born in Yamagata Prefecture in 1956. He studied art at Nihon University. In 1990, he published his first picture book, *Melody*. In 1997, he won the Shōgakukan Children's Publishing Culture Prize for *The Lying Moon*. In 1999, Arai's *Journey of Riddles* received the Special Award at the Bologna Book Fair. He won the Astrid Lindgren Memorial Award, the highest international award in children's literature, in 2005. In 2009, he won the JBBY Prize for *The Sun Organ*. In 2012, *It's Morning — Let's Open A Window* received the Sankei Children's Book Award.

David Boyd is Assistant Professor of Japanese at the University of North Carolina at Charlotte. His translations have appeared in *Monkey Business International, Granta*, and *Words Without Borders,* among other publications.

Library of Congress Cataloging-in-Publication Data

Names: **Osada, Hiroshi**, 1939-2015, author. |
Arai, Ryōji, 1956- illustrator. | **Boyd, David** (David G.), translator.
Title: *Every color of light* / written by **Hiroshi Osada** ;
illustrated by **Ryōji Arai** ; translated by **David Boyd**.
Other titles: *Kyō wa sora ni marui tsuki*. English
Description: First English language edition. |
Brooklyn, NY : Enchanted Lion Books, 2020. |
"First published in Japan in 2011 by Kodansha Ltd., Tokyo." |
Audience: Ages 4-10. | Audience: Grades 2-3. |
Summary: Illustrations and easy-to-read, rhyming text depict nature
darkened by a brief rainstorm then, at sunset, colors brighten, rain drips
like crystals, and the bright white moon shines as we fall asleep.
Identifiers: LCCN 2020008249 | ISBN 9781592702916 (hardcover)
Subjects: CYAC: Stories in rhyme. | Nature--Fiction. |
Rain and rainfall--Fiction. | Bedtime--Fiction. | Color--Fiction.
Classification: LCC PZ8.3.O775 Eve 2020 | DDC [E]--dc23
LC record available at https://lccn.loc.gov/2020008249

www.enchantedlion.com

First English language edition published in 2020 by Enchanted Lion Books
67 West St, Suite 403, Brooklyn, NY 11222

Book design by Eugenia Mello.

A CIP record is on file with the Library of Congress
ISBN: 978-1-59270-291-6

Printed in 2020 by Grafiche AZ, Verona